Spaghetti in a Hot Dog Bun

Having the Courage to Be Who You Are

Written by Maria Dismondy
Illustrations by Kim Shaw

Spaghetti in a Hot Dog Bun:
Having the Courage to Be Who You Are

Copyright © 2008 by Maria Cini Dismondy
Illustrations by Kim Shaw
Twelfth Printing 2016
Printed in the United States of America

Acknowledgements

Thank you to my family and friends for your endless support. I am appreciative for the guidance of those at Nelson Publishing and Marketing and to my editor, Kathy Hiatt, for helping bring this project to life. —M.D.

To the love of my life, Dave... proof that
dreams really do come true.

M.D.

To mom and dad, for supporting the dreams
of your daughters with love and compassion.

K.S.

The delicious smell of breakfast filled the air as Lucy's grandpa handed her a plate. Lucy smeared ketchup on her toast. She turned to her grandpa and said, "Papa Gino, Harriet said she's never heard of ketchup on toast. Her family uses butter and jelly."

"It's okay, not everyone likes the same thing, Lucy. It doesn't mean one person is right or wrong. We're all different. What a boring world it would be if we were all exactly alike! Do you remember what's really important?" Papa Gino asked.

"Yes, Papa. Even if we are different from others on the outside, we all have a heart with feelings on the inside."

"That's my girl! Remember, when you treat others with love and kindness, you are doing the right thing," Papa Gino replied.

On the school bus, Lucy and her friend Harriet pulled out some paper and crayons. Sitting across from them was Ralph. As usual, Ralph sat alone, staring out the window. He looked over at them and rolled his eyes.

In the classroom, Lucy sat down near the teacher. Ralph carelessly hurried over and tripped on Lucy's foot. Before long, he was glaring at her.

Ralph whispered, "Woof! I can't see the book with this poodle in front of me."
Lucy could hear him giggling behind her. *Oh no, why did it have to be me?*
she wondered.

FRIENDSHIP WEEK: SHARE A SMILE!

Angela

DAVID

During lunch, Harriet shouted one of her silly jokes over the other children's voices. As the girls ate, their bellies shook with laughter.

Across the table, Ralph hollered, "Yuck. That's the disgusting smell. Whoever heard of eating spaghetti in a hot dog bun?"

Tony and the other children at the table turned away from Ralph, shaking their heads. Ralph continued, "Poor little Lucy with her hair so poofy!" Tears filled Lucy's eyes, and she began to cry.

On the way home, Lucy thought about what had happened. *Maybe Ralph is mean to me because he thinks being different is bad. I wish he would stop teasing me.*

Slowly, Lucy stepped off the bus. "How was your day?" Papa Gino asked. "Fine," she mumbled. Papa reached over and pulled a crayon out of her hair. "How did this happen?" he asked. Lucy didn't say a word.

That night, as Papa Gino tucked Lucy into bed, he asked, "Is everything all right at school?" Lucy rolled over. He sat down and whispered, "Always remember, if something's not right, we can work on fixing it together." *It's not that easy,* thought Lucy. *How do I stop Ralph from teasing me? How can he have a heart and be so mean?*

Lucy had a hard time falling asleep, worrying what would happen tomorrow.

The following day, Lucy was surprised to find Ralph leaving her alone, until...
Lucy took the bag Ralph handed her. Inside were dog bones with a note that
read: Lucy, Lucy, eats stinky food that puts us in a big, bad mood. Lucy, Lucy,
hair shaped like a cone, here's a treat for you— a yummy dog bone!

The beating of Lucy's heart was so loud she knew everyone around her could hear it. "Stop! It hurts my feelings when you do this, Ralph," Lucy said. "Please stop!" Ralph turned and walked away.

It was recess time, and Lucy played alone. She didn't want to tell her teacher about Ralph. She was afraid of being a tattletale. Lucy wished Papa Gino was there to help. *What should I do?* she asked herself over and over. The bell rang as recess ended.

"Heeeeelllllppppp!" cried a child off in the distance. Tony yelled, "Ralph got himself stuck at the top of the monkey bars. It's the funniest thing I've ever seen!"

"This is my chance, I'll go tell Ralph how mean he really is--M-E-A-N, mean!" Lucy stomped off toward the monkey bars.

When she reached Ralph, Lucy paused. She looked him in the eye and said, "What you did was *so* mean!" Standing before Ralph, Lucy could hear her papa's words. Ralph *did* have a heart with feelings.

In that moment, Lucy decided what she would do. She saw tears in Ralph's eyes. He hesitated to move and whispered, "I'm scared." Lucy reached out and said, "Here, take my hand," and she helped him down.

The two walked back to the classroom without saying a word.

As the bus pulled up to Lucy's stop, Ralph reached over and handed her a picture. Lucy was amazed by what she saw. "Thanks," she muttered softly.

After she got off the bus, Lucy smiled and said, "Papa, there's this boy Ralph who was really mean to me. Today he was in trouble, and I helped him."

Papa Gino hugged Lucy and replied, "That took a lot of courage. It wasn't the easiest thing to do. You chose to treat others the way you want to be treated. I'm so proud of you, Lucy."

As they walked home, she asked him what was for dinner. When Papa Gino said spaghetti, Lucy knew immediately what she would have for lunch the next day...

her favorite sandwich, spaghetti in a hot dog bun.

Maria Dismondy is an award-winning author specializing in books about challenges children face, such as bullying, a topic close to her heart. Maria's own childhood experience inspired her first book, *Spaghetti in a Hot Dog Bun*. Several books later, Maria continues to inspire children with her messages of courage, kindness, and confidence. Having earned degrees in child development and education, Maria taught elementary school for more than a decade. She resigned from the classroom and works to spread the empowering messages in her books to schools nationwide. Maria lives in southeast Michigan with her husband Dave and her three book-loving children.

Kim Shaw is an illustrator, an art educator, and a lifelong learner of all things art. Other books illustrated by Kim include *Darcy Daisy and the Firefly Festival*, *The Crayon Kids' Art Adventure*, and *The Juice Box Bully*. In her free time, Kim enjoys Lake Michigan, camping, and foraging for mushrooms with her lovely husband, Andy. Kim has a great love for nature, her incredible daughters, and the good people of Kalamazoo, MI, and looks forward to expanding her knowledge of all these things through art and love.

Spaghetti in a Hot Dog Bun is now a musical!

Stars Within Reach Productions creates, produces, and provides access to professional theater for young and family audiences nationwide. To bring the production to your school, visit www.starswithinreachproductions.com.

You are out of this world SPECIAL!

1. Be proud.
2. Love yourself.
3. Have courage.
4. Practice giving.
5. Make each day count.
6. Celebrate differences.
7. Spread kindness.
8. Share a smile.
9. Forgive.
10. Never give up.